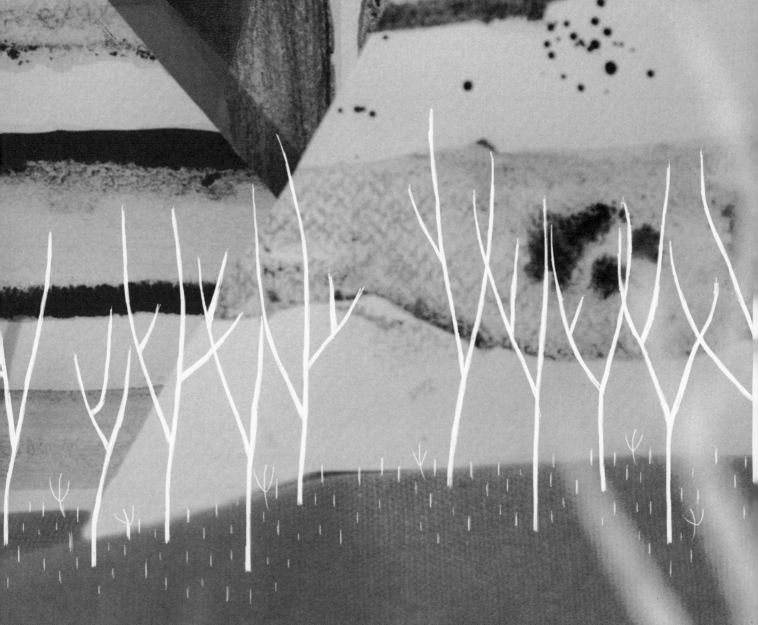

the PERFECT TREE

Chloe Bonfield

RP | KIDS
PHILADELPHIA • LONDON

Books published by Running Press are available at special discounts for bulk purchases in the United States by corporations, institutions, and other organizations. For more information, please contact the Special Markets Department at the Perseus Books Group, 2300 Chestnut Street, Suite 200, Philadelphia, PA 19103, or call (800) 810-4145, ext. 5000, or e-mail special.markets@perseusbooks.com.

ISBN 978-0-7624-5586-7
Library of Congress Control Number: 2015940929

9 8 7 6 5 4 3 2 1
Digit on the right indicates the number of this printing

Designed by T.L. Bonaddio
Edited by Marlo Scrimizzi
Typography: Bookeyed Nelson, Paper Cute, and Scrimshaw

Published by Running Press Kids
An Imprint of Running Press Book Publishers
A Member of the Perseus Books Group
2300 Chestnut Street
Philadelphia, PA 19103–4371

Visit us on the web!
www.runningpress.com/rpkids

FOR BELLA AND ALBIE

Once, a boy named Jack went on a journey to find the perfect tree.
Not to climb, not to draw, and definitely not to hug.

No, Jack wanted a perfect tree to chop.
A perfect tree to hack! A perfect tree to stack.

The trees he saw were too wide,

too spooky,   too silly,   or too familiar.

Jack reached a hill and climbed to the top.
No perfect trees were there.

He climbed down the other side.
Nothing.

The perfect tree was really very hard to find.

Jack wandered into a dark corner
of the forest, and his heart began to sink.
And then he heard . . .

TAP, TAP, TAP . . . TAP, TA

"I've been watching you,"
said a woodpecker.
"Come with me,
I'll show you the
perfect tree."

As fast as an arrow, the woodpecker flew through the leaves.

"Here we are," said the woodpecker.
"Just you wait and see what happens next."

TAP
TAP
TAP
TAP

Jack's heart soared as birds and feathers filled the air.
They tickled his face and tangled in his hair.

TWITCH,

TWITCH,

TWITCH . . .

TWITCH, TWITCH, TWITCH,
said a nosy squirrel's nose.
"You think that's a sight to see?
Come with me and *I'll* show you the perfect tree."

As swift as a gymnast,
the squirrel flipped through the trees . . .

. . . and landed in
front of a great big oak.
"Follow me!"
said the squirrel.

Jack couldn't believe what he saw inside the oak tree! There were enough acorns and berries to last all winter, maybe more!

CLICK, CLICK, CLICK . . .

Outside, a soft shadow with
eight long legs scurried along.

"Don't be afraid of little old me. Have you seen my perfect tree?" said a spider.

Jack took the end of the spider's web
and they glided among the trees.

High up in a spindly tree hung a magnificent web,
with jewels hanging from every strand.

DRIP, DRIP, DRIP . . .

DRIP,

DRIP,

DRIP.

The rain began to pour.
"You had better run for cover!" said the spider.
As Jack ran, he looked for the perfect shelter
to keep him dry. And what did he see?

Jack could finally see
this was the perfect tree.

But as Jack looked at the woodpecker,
squirrel, and spider, he remembered the trees he saw
that day. They were all so special.
"Every tree in the forest is perfect," said Jack.
So he put down his ax, for he needed it no more.
Then Jack said good-bye to his new friends as
he made his way home.

The next day,
Jack went on another journey
to find the perfect tree.
No, not a perfect tree to chop!

A perfect tree to climb,
a perfect tree to draw, and most of all...

A perfect tree to love.